Monkey Business

Sam stood u

Hunched ...ders.

Put his hands in his pockets.

"That's okay, Kiddo."

He sloped off towards the door.

"I'm Mogo, the chimp who does what he does when it has to be done." He turned and gave a wave. "Right here in the now, I'm off to find the Loch Ness Monster."

When he looked back, the class was following behind. All in their Chimp Mogo masks!

More *brilliant* Young Hippo School stories:

The Grott Street Gang
Terry Deary

Nightingale News
Odette Elliot

Pet Swapping Day
Whizz Bang and the Crocodile Room
Susan Gates

A Parsnip Called Val
Sylvia Green

School for Dragons
Ann Jungman

Class Four's Wild Week
Malcolm Yorke

Have you tried these other great Young Hippos by Kara May?

Emily H and the Enormous Tarantula
Emily H and the Stranger in the Castle
Emily H Turns Detective

Big Puss, Little Mouse

KARA MAY

Monkey Business

Illustrated by Sami Sweeten

JB

For Sam R-B.

Scholastic Children's Books,
Commonwealth House, 1-19 New Oxford Street,
London WC1A 1NU, UK
a division of Scholastic Ltd
London ~ New York ~ Toronto ~ Sydney ~ Auckland

Published in the UK by Scholastic Ltd, 1998

Text copyright © Kara May, 1998
Illustrations copyright © Sami Sweeten, 1998

ISBN 0 590 11125 6

Typeset by Backup Creative Services, Dorset
Printed by Cox & Wyman Ltd, Reading, Berks

2 4 6 8 10 9 7 5 3 1

Chapter 1

Another school day!

Groan! Groan! went Sam.

Not that he didn't like school. He did. Most of the time. But today he felt like doing something different. Something he'd never done before. Like:

Go exploring in the jungle

Take off in a spaceship
Or maybe—

But here was Mr Brett.

Sam made a dash for his chair. His eyes went to Mr Brett's socks. He could tell what mood Mr Brett was in by the socks he had on:

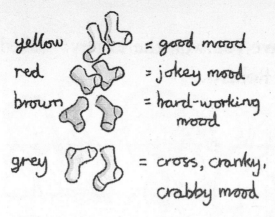

yellow = good mood
red = jokey mood
brown = hard-working mood

grey = cross, cranky, crabby mood

But today...! Sam stared. Orange socks with purple spots! Mr Brett had never worn those before. He was trying to work out what mood they meant when Mr Brett tapped on his desk.

"I've got some news for you," he said.

"Have you won the lottery?" asked Andy Roberts.

"Are you getting married to Miss Hurst?" piped up Jasu Sharma.

Mr Brett turned pink but he didn't say a word. With that look on his face, thought Sam, he didn't have to – it was enough to turn the giggles into graveyard quiet.

"Now you've simmered down," he said at last, "the news is that G. G.

Higgins is coming to talk to you next Friday."

"G. G. Higgins. Wow!" glowed Sam.

He wasn't the only one to feel excited. G. G. Higgins wrote stories about Chimp Mogo. Sam looked towards the Book Corner. There were posters of the stories on the wall – eight so far.

The stories were all adventures full of danger for Chimp Mogo – not that he was scared, not ever. Sam wasn't much of a reader but he'd read them all and he couldn't wait for the next one to come out.

"If it was me who was writing the next one, I'd be waiting for ever!" He was more of a plonker at writing stories than reading. The longest story he'd written went:

One day I went to the beach. It was hot. I went for a swim. I went and looked at the seaweed. There was a crab.

He'd done a great drawing of the crab but to think up the words was like squeezing toothpaste from the bottom of the tube. He was sure it wasn't like that for G. G. Higgins.

"What's G. G. Higgins like?" he asked.

"No one seems to know. It's a mystery," said Mr Brett. "Not even the people who publish the stories know if G. G. Higgins is a he or a she."

"I think G. G.'s for Greg Griffin," said Sam.

"I think it's for Gina Gillian," said Jasu.

Sam sat, frowning. There was a puzzle here, he thought. "It's ace that G. G. Higgins is coming, Mr Brett, but if he/she's a mystery, why would he/she come and talk to us?"

Jasu grinned. "I know why. Because Alton Juniors is the best school in the world."

"And we're the best class in it!"

Mr Brett held up his hand for silence. "We'll have Ms Macaby coming to see if a zoo's got loose in here." (Ms Macaby was the Head.) "Now let's get on with some spelling."

Sam groaned.

He wasn't the only one!

From all the class it was:

groan! groan!

"Spelling first. Then sums," said Mr Brett. "Then after break…"

"What?" asked Sam.

"Wait and see," said Mr Brett.

Sam grinned to himself.

First there was Mr Brett's never-worn-before orange and purple socks.

Then the news about G. G. Higgins.

Next the G. G. Higgins mystery.

Now what?

Today was turning out to be different.

Not a Groan! Groan! school day after all!

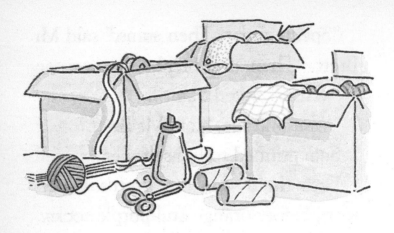

Chapter 2

When they got in after break, Mr Brett was waiting for them. On his desk were some large cardboard boxes. He was drumming his fingers on them and tapping his feet.

Orange socks with purple spots = fidgety mood, thought Sam. He peered forward. Mr Brett was taking things from the boxes.

"To make the most of G. G. Higgins's visit, I thought we'd do some projects about Chimp Mogo.

"I've got some ideas," went on Mr Brett. "But I hope you clever lot will have some ideas too. For the next week, we'll be sleeping, eating, *dreaming* Chimp Mogo."

"That's okay by me, Kiddo."

Mr Brett jumped as if a fire cracker had gone off. "Who ... what! ... who said that?" He looked round, his eyes on full alert.

Oh oh! Me and my big mouth, thought Sam. He'd never let on, not to anyone, but he'd made up his own Chimp Mogo voice. Now it had just popped out.

"It was me, Mr Brett," he said.

To his one hundred per cent surprise, Mr Brett asked him to do it again.

Oh flip! he thought. Not just Mr Brett, *everyone* was looking at him. Sam felt himself going not pink but red. He wanted to get up and run. But Chimp Mogo wouldn't run. He'd do what he had to do!

"That's okay by me, Kiddo," he said once more.

Sam grinned. This was fun. He was getting into it now. "I've got a Chimp Mogo walk too!" he said.

He put his hands in his pockets.
Hunched up his shoulders.
Then he sloped around the classroom.

"Hi there," he said. "I'm Mogo. The chimp who does what he does when it has to be done."

"How do you do it, Sam?"

"Sit down! All of you! At once!" said Mr Brett. "If Ms Macaby were to walk in now…"

No need to say more! The thought was enough to send the class back to their places. "For our first project," he went on, "we're going to make a life-size Chimp Mogo."

"We don't need to make one, we've got Sam. We could dress him up and stuff him," chortled Andy Roberts.

Sam winced. "Ha! ha!" he said, and went to look in the boxes.

He picked out a large yellow hat and put it on. "If we cut the brim off, it'll be like Chimp Mogo's hat. Thanks," he added, as Mr Brett handed him the scissors.

The class had made models before. But this was the best ever! It was as if Chimp Mogo was coming alive in front of them.

Last of all, Mr Brett attached the face mask that they'd made.

"It's like Chimp Mogo's here in our very classroom," said Sam. "It's like he's come to school. Not that he'd want to," he added. "He's much too busy having exciting adventures."

"I don't know about that. He might learn something," said Mr Brett.

Sam hunched his shoulders.

Put his hands in his pockets.

"When it comes to school, count me out, Kiddo!"

But from then on, to his surprise, and for the first time ever, Sam found he couldn't wait to get to school. He didn't go Groan! Groan! once. Even everyday lessons seemed fun with Chimp Mogo in the classroom. And more often than not they did Chimp Mogo projects, getting ready for G. G. Higgins's visit.

They did paintings of his adventures and put them on the wall (Andy Roberts's idea).

They read bits of their favourite
stories to each other (Mr Brett's idea).

Sam read to Jasu from *Chimp Mogo
and Wizard Wozot*, which was more
funny than scary.

He chose the bit where Chimp Mogo gets to hear how the Wizard is putting spells on people who won't hand him over their money. Well, Chimp Mogo isn't having that!

Mr Brett came over to listen.

"Well read, Sam. You didn't stumble over the words once."

Sam grinned to himself. He could have said (but he didn't!) that he knew most of it by heart.

Now it was Jasu's turn to read. She was going to read from *Wizard Wozot* too, but later in the story.

"I've got a better idea," she said. "Instead of reading from the book, we could act out some of the story as if it was a play."

"It's okay with me, Kiddo," said Sam in his Chimp Mogo voice. He nodded towards Mr Brett. "But what about The Teach? No time like the now. Let's put it to him."

"Fingers crossed he says yes," said Jasu.

"I bet he does!" grinned Sam. Mr Brett was wearing his yellow = good mood socks!

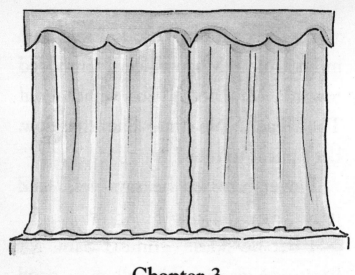

Chapter 3

"A play? I don't see why not," said Mr Brett.

"Nice one, Sam! Your yellow = good mood sock code works!" Sam said to himself. All the class were keen on Jasu's Play Idea and wanted to be in it too.

"I don't see why not," said Mr Brett

again. "First, let's give our play a name."

Andy Roberts (who else!) shouted out, "*Chimp Mogo Teaches Wizard Wozot a Lesson He Never Forgets.* No one'll think of a better one than that!"

"You want to see a shrink to shrink your big head, Andy," said Jasu.

Everyone laughed, even Andy.

"All right, simmer down!" said Mr Brett. "We've got lots to do to get ready for our play. To begin with, let's decide who'll be who. How about

Sam as Chimp Mogo and Jasu as Wizard Wozot? The rest of you know the story well enough to be the other characters."

At last they sorted out who was to be who.

"Now you know your characters, you can work out what they say as the play goes along. But there is ONE BIG MUST," said Mr Brett.

"You MUST listen to whoever is speaking," he went on. "If you all start yapping at once, all we'll get is a mess and not a play. Okay?"

"I'll give you fifteen minutes to get ready. You can make yourselves whatever props you think your character needs. Use anything in the classroom. It's up to you. If you want to dress up, use the things from the boxes."

Jasu found a tablecloth. "It'll do for Wizard Wozot's cloak," she said.

Then she rolled up some thick paper and stuck it together down the side. "This can be his hat. All I need is a ruler for a wand. What about you, Sam?"

Sam was standing by himself, trying to get rid of the concrete mixer that was churning in his tummy. He'd been all for Jasu's idea at first. But now it came to it...

What if he couldn't think of what to say?

What if he couldn't do his Chimp Mogo voice?

He knew what! Andy Roberts would laugh himself silly. And he, Sam, would be the joke!

Still, if he was going to make a prat of himself, no time like the now! He went and rummaged in the boxes. He knew he wouldn't find a yellow and white jacket like Chimp Mogo's but any big jacket would do.

"Borrow mine," said Mr Brett. "And I'm sure just this once, Chimp Mogo will lend you his hat."

"Thanks, Chimp Mogo," said Sam. "I'll do my best to do you proud."

Sam couldn't wait for the play to start.

The concrete mixer in his tummy had turned into a shaken-up bottle of Coke and he was fizzing with excitement.

At last everyone was ready.

At a nod from Mr Brett, Jasu went striding forward. "I am Wizard Wozot!" she roared out in a mean and frightening voice.

Sam crouched down in the Book Corner. But he wasn't Sam now, he was Chimp Mogo, biding his time until he could sort out the money-grubbing Wizard Wozot.

Chimp Mogo Teaches Wizard Wozot a Lesson He Never Forgets

A PLAY

Characters:

Chimp Mogo

Wizard Wozot

People of the town of Cocklewidge:

Willy Ball, a football manager

Ginny Burger, a dinner lady

Fred Sprint, a newspaper boy

Mrs Hare, a mother of six children

The little Hares

And lots of others.

The scene:

A street in Cocklewidge where some Cocklewidgers are having a protest march. Led by Ginny Burger and Willy Ball, they carry banners: *We Say No To Wizard Wozot, Down With Wozot, Wozot's Not Getting Our Money,* etc.

The action:

The Cocklewidgers stand together, trying to look brave as Wizard Wozot paces furiously about.

WOZOT: How dare you defy me, Cocklewidgers! How dare you not do as I say!

COCKLEWIDGERS: We've had enough of you, Wozot.

WOZOT: I ask you again: hand over your money!

COCKLEWIDGERS: You can ask all you want, the answer is NO!

WOZOT: I'll give you one more chance—

GINNY BURGER: The answer's still NO, Wozot.

WILLY BALL: That's it, Ginny, you tell him!

MRS HARE: I'll tell him too, and so will my little Hares!

LITTLE HARES: Yeah, we'll tell you, Wozot!

FRED SPRINT: I've had to work for my money. Delivering newspapers at the crack of dawn is no joke, I can tell you.

COCKLEWIDGERS: You're not getting a pound, not a *p* out of us.

WOZOT: You'll be sorry—

COCKLEWIDGERS: No, we won't!

WOZOT: Oh yes you will!

COCKLEWIDGERS: Oh no we won't.

WOZOT: You verminillious Cocklewidgers, I told you what I'd do to you if you didn't hand over your money.

GINNY BURGER: (*whispers*) Don't let him see you're scared.

WILLY BALL: (*whispers*) Let's show him what we're made of!

WOZOT: Prepare to suffer the terrible fate I warned you about. My wand is programmed to all sorts of spells. Spells to turn you from Cocklewidgers into toads and bats and squeaky mice and spiders. (*He strides about.*) It's too late to ask for mercy.

COCKLEWIDGERS: We weren't going to!

WOZOT: Breathe your last as Cocklewidgers. No one can save you from being toaderized, baterized, mouserized, spiderized. I raise my wand and—

Enter Chimp Mogo

CHIMP MOGO: Hold it right there, Wozot.

COCKLEWIDGERS: It's Chimp Mogo!

WOZOT: (*scared*) Chimp Mogo!

CHIMP MOGO: The chimp who does what he does when it has to be done. You got it in one, Wozot. (*To Cocklewidgers*) Best stand back and leave the Wiz to me.

WILLY BALL: You heard what Chimp Mogo said. Over here, Cocklewidgers!

(*The Cocklewidgers draw back.*)

CHIMP MOGO: I've been hearing things about you, Wozot. Thought I'd drop by and check you out.

WOZOT: (*trembling*) I've heard of you, of course. Pleased to meet you, I'm sure.

CHIMP MOGO: You don't look too sure to me. You've gone as white as a spook with the gut-ache.

WOZOT: (*very scared*) L ... l ... look, I've n-nothing against y-you. Just go away and l-let me get on.

CHIMP MOGO: (*sits down*) I'll stay, thanks all the same, Wozot.

WOZOT: I thought you called everyone Kiddo...

CHIMP MOGO: Just my friends, Wozot.

WOZOT: Ah! (*going*) I've just remembered I've got a spell pot on the boil.

CHIMP MOGO: You're going no place no time – not till you promise not to put spells on these Cocklewidgers or anyone else unless they say so.

WOZOT: I'm not doing that! And you can't make me! If you try to—

CHIMP MOGO: *I* wouldn't try to, Wozot. (*He looks meaningfully at the Cocklewidgers.*) But the fire-breathing dragon behind you might!

(*The Cocklewidgers give a dragon-like roar. Wozot spins round to look. Chimp Mogo leaps forward and grabs the wand from the off-guard Wozot.*)

CHIMP MOGO: You fell for that one, Wozot!

COCKLEWIDGERS: Not so clever, Wozot!

WOZOT: (*furious*) Give it back. Give me back my wand!

CHIMP MOGO: No can do, Wozot. You and your wand are a menace.

COCKLEWIDGERS: Hear, hear!

CHIMP MOGO: You've used the spells in it to get money from people. What d'you say to that?

WOZOT: Er...

CHIMP MOGO: Let's see how you like being on the other end of your wand! (*He presses a button on the wand.*)

FRED SPRINT: Look! Wozot's eyes! They're going bulgy!

WOZOT: I'm being toaderized! Help! Help!

COCKLEWIDGERS: Serve you right, Wozot!

LITTLE HARES: His hands are turning into flippers!

WILLY BALL: His toes are getting webbed!

MRS HARE: You've got yourself a big fat round toad tum, Wozot.

LITTLE HARES: Yeah, a big fat round toad tum!

WOZOT: (*his voice is getting croaky*) I don't want to be a toad!

COCKLEWIDGERS: Croak! Croak! Croak!

CHIMP MOGO: Maybe you'd sooner be a – let's see! (*He presses another button on the wand.*)

COCKLEWIDGERS: He's turned into a mouse! Squeak! Squeak! Eek! Eek!

WOZOT: (*squeaks*) I don't want to be a mouse!

CHIMP MOGO: Then how about a spider?

WOZOT: Not a spider. I'm scared of spiders!

CHIMP MOGO: Then I'll do you a favour and let you stay a mouse.

WOZOT: (*begging*) Chimp Mogo, please let me be me again.

CHIMP MOGO: Even if I wanted to, I don't know how.

WOZOT: It's the last spell on the wand. It turns things back into what they were before they got spellerized.

CHIMP MOGO: (*going*) Thanks, Wozot. I'm off to de-spell all those people you toaderized and so on.

LITTLE HARES: The Wiz turned our dad into a bat! It'll be great to have him back as Dad again.

COCKLEWIDGERS: We'll never forget what you've done for us, Chimp Mogo.

CHIMP MOGO: I just do what I do when it has to be done.

WOZOT: (*running after them*) Wait! What about me?

CHIMP MOGO: You're last on the de-spell list, Wozot.

WOZOT: (*grovel, grovel*) You won't forget me? Please, Chimp Mogo.

CHIMP MOGO: I said I'd de-spell you, Wozot.

CHIMP MOGO & COCKLEWIDGERS: Chimp Mogo does what he does when it has to be done and means what he says when he says it!

Sam took off his Chimp Mogo hat.

Jasu took off her Wizard hat.

"The End," they said.

The class clapped and cheered each other. No one clapped and cheered louder than Mr Brett.

"You were brilliant, all of you! This play's too good not to be shown again. I'll have a think about what we can do with it later. But for now, well done! Bravo!"

Sam took off Mr Brett's jacket and

Chimp Mogo's hat. He was just Sam now but he still felt great. He'd been jelly-shake scared he'd mess the play up, but he'd taken the risk and gone for it anyway.

And he was glad he had!

Still wearing his Willy Ball football manager moustache, Andy Roberts came over and gave him the thumbs up. "You should be in the movies, Sam. You're good enough."

"Thanks a bunch, Kiddo!"

Much more of this, thought Sam, and Andy wouldn't be the only big-head in the class!

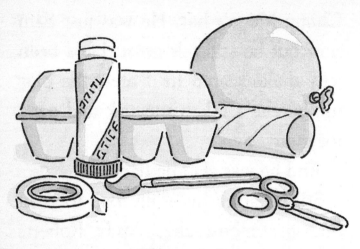

Chapter 5

After the excitement of the play, the rest of the week went whizzing by. It was as if Wizard Wozot had put a spell on it to speed it up, thought Sam. Tomorrow was G. G. Higgins Day.

"Not bad," he said, looking at the Chimp Mogo face mask he was making. They were all making them so that G. G. Higgins would find a classful of Chimp Mogos when he/she walked in. (Another idea from Clever Clogs Andy Roberts but, Sam had to admit, it was a good one.)

Sam couldn't wait to try the mask on.

"Not now," said Mr Brett. "Write your names on the back and put them in the cupboard till tomorrow. Now, about tomorrow…"

"We'll be like angels, Mr Brett."

"That'll be a change," he grinned.

"Ms Macaby's coming to meet G. G. Higgins too. So how do we want the classroom?"

"Spick and span!"

Sam went to tidy the Book Corner.

He flipped through the pages of the Chimp Mogo stories, and all that night he dreamed of Chimp Mogo and his adventures.

When he woke up he thought he'd dreamt of G. G. Higgins, too, but he couldn't remember what. Not long now, and he'd be meeting THE MYSTERY AUTHOR for real. Too excited to walk, he ran all the way to school.

I'm early, he thought. This must be a record. But where was Mr Brett?

Five minutes late, Mr Brett rushed in.

"Let's get on. And not a word about G. G. Higgins. Time enough for that after break!" he puffed.

He raced through the register as if he had a train to catch.

Then he told them to get out their spelling books.

Five minutes later it was, "Do your sums."

"Which is it? Sums or spelling?" asked Andy.

Mr Brett didn't seem to hear. He just paced about the classroom and every now and then he gave nervy little jumps.

What's up with him? thought Sam. Oh oh! So that's it! Mr Brett was wearing the orange socks with purple spots! Orange socks with purple spots = fidgety mood! I hope he gets himself together. It's not long now till G. G. Higgins comes.

BZZZZ!

There it was, the buzzer for break. Sam went to join the rush for the door. Then he remembered the Chimp Mogo face masks. "They're still in the cupboard, Mr Brett. We were meant to have them on for G. G. Higgins."

"So you were. I forgot. Too late now."

Mr Brett went to whoosh Sam off, but Sam wasn't giving up that easily. They'd gone to all the trouble of making the face masks – so now they should wear them!

"I don't mind missing break. I could put them out on the tables," Sam said.

"You're a big Chimp Mogo fan, aren't you, Sam?"

Sam nodded. "We click somehow. When I'm being Chimp Mogo, it's as if I really am him."

"That's how it seems to me, too. The first time I heard you, I thought he'd walked into the classroom."

"The stories make him seem so real. I can't wait for the next one. There hasn't been a new one for ages. I'm going to ask G. G. Higgins what it'll be about—" Sam broke off. Mr Brett was looking at him as if he'd turned into a ghost.

"Must dash!" Mr Brett croaked, and scarpered.

It's those socks, they seem to do something to him! thought Sam. He grinned at the Chimp Mogo model. "Soon we'll all look like you!" he said.

Before he set the masks out on the tables, he tried on each one and showed it to Chimp Mogo. He was having such fun it seemed break had just begun when the class came charging back, led by Andy Roberts.

Sam saw at once by their faces that something was up.

"We've just seen Ms Macaby," said Andy.

Sam's heart thudded to his feet. "Isn't G. G. Higgins coming after all?" he asked, trying to keep the choking feeling from his throat.

But it was Mr Brett who'd caused the upset. There'd been a sudden emergency and he'd had to go home.

"Ms Macaby was in a state, I can tell you," said Jasu. "She says we've got to be quiet and sit still till G. G. Higgins comes."

"Whew! Thank goodness he *is* coming," said Sam. "Too bad Mr Brett has to miss out. But let's do everything as if he was here."

"G. G. Higgins!" they breathed together.

"Quickly, everyone. Chimp Mogo masks on!" cried Sam.

Chapter 6

"Hi there one and all! I'm G. G. Higgins!"

He looks just like a Greg Griffin, Sam smiled to himself. G. G. Higgins had a wild mop of red hair and a bushy red beard. He was wearing a red velvet jacket and bright green trousers.

"You're a lovely looking lot!" he said

in a loud and booming voice. "It's more like a wildlife park than a classroom," he grinned. "And that's the way I like it!"

"So do we, Mr Higgins!"

"Call me GGH."

Then he saw their model of Chimp Mogo. "How you doing, Mogo?" he asked and went over and shook him by the hand.

"He's not real, GGH. We made him."

"You didn't?"

"We did!"

"And what genius did these?" he asked, looking at their drawings of Chimp Mogo's adventures.

"We did those, too."

"And guess what else!" bubbled Jasu. "We did a play about Chimp Mogo and Wizard Wozot!"

They told GGH about it.

"You know what I'm thinking?" GGH said.

They couldn't wait to find out!

"I'm thinking," said GGH, "you should do this play again so all the school can see it and all the parents too, with proper scenery and costumes."

"Wow! Do you think we'd be good enough?"

"Can birds fly and lizards squiggle? Of course you would!" beamed GGH.

It was Andy Roberts (who else!) who asked what everyone was thinking: "If we do our play, will you come and see it, GGH?"

GGH put his hand on his heart. "I promise," he said. "It's an honour to be asked. Thanks a million. And thanks a million for all the trouble you've gone to for me today. But now—!" He suddenly smacked his hand with his fist. "It's time for the nitty-gritty, it's time I told you why I'm here."

"Shall I give it to you straight?" asked GGH.

"Then I won't beat about the bush or mumble round the jungle – I'm in trouble," he said with a deeply serious face. "Trouble with a big T. And so's Chimp Mogo."

Chimp Mogo and GGH in trouble! This was serious.

Sam took off his face mask.

So did the others.

"I write about Chimp Mogo and his adventures, as you know. I see them clearly in my mind as if they're happening in front of me. All I do is write them down."

So that's how he does it! thought Sam.

"But for ages now, when I see Chimp Mogo, do you know what he's doing?"

"He's watching TV. All day. All night! There he is, gawping like a blob of potato sat on a couch. He's turning into a couch potato!"

"A couch potato!" gasped Sam. "That's impossible."

"I wish it was!" groaned GGH.

"But that's awful!" Sam knew how Chimp Mogo would feel, stuck indoors all the time. "He likes having exciting and fun and dangerous adventures. He'll hate being a couch potato. It'll be a fate worse than being strangled by the twenty-headed octopus on Planet X!"

GGH sighed. "He escaped from the octopus. But I fear he won't escape from being a couch potato unless he has another adventure."

why doesn't he?

"Because I can't think of one for him to have!" GGH pointed towards the Book Corner. "When it comes to adventures, Chimp Mogo's done it all."

Sam saw at once what GGH meant.

Chimp Mogo had had adventures all over the world, in the past, in the present, and in the future too.

"The way things look now, my next book will be *Chimp Mogo Turns Couch Potato*." GGH pulled a face. "No thrills or fun in that! Would any of you want to read it?"

Sam could see everyone was thinking the same as him: No way!

"I had the word you were a clever lot. That's why I'm here, to see if you can give me an adventure for Chimp Mogo. Any offers?"

GGH looked around the class.

In reply all he got was:

SILENCE!

Chapter 7

Sam sat with a frown on his face, thinking. All round him he could feel everyone else thinking too, racking their brain cells for an adventure to save Chimp Mogo from his couch potato fate.

"I'd better own up, GGH," he said at last. "I'm no good at making up adventures. In fact, I've only had one adventure in all my life."

To his surprise, GGH perked up at once. "Let's hear it. Roll it past me."

Me and my big mouth again, Sam inwardly groaned. The sooner he got this over, the better.

"It was only half an adventure, really," he said. "I was on holiday in Scotland with Mum and Dad. On the last day we went to Loch Ness. I went off for a walk by myself."

As he spoke, he could see it as if he were there now. The great murky lake, big as a sea. The wind whipping over the water.

Then, suddenly, there it was!

Something rising up out of the waves.

A head!
A long neck!
And then—

"Then Dad shouted for me and it went. If only he hadn't shouted then," said Sam, "because I'm sure it was the Loch Ness Monster, and no one's ever seen it, not all of it – because it lives in the deepest depths of the lake." He broke off, then rushed on, "If anyone could find it, it'd be Chimp Mogo! It could be his next adventure!"

Sam's mind was racing fast. Ideas were coming one after the other. "What could happen is this:

"Chimp Mogo gets to hear some greedy money-grubbers are after the monster. They're going to put him in a zoo and make people pay to see him so they'll get rich. Chimp Mogo fears the monster will die of a broken heart if he's taken from the loch—"

Sam's burst of ideas had run out. He felt like a balloon that had been pricked. "That's as far as I've got," he said.

"It's far enough and further! It's brain-stoppingly brilliant! Chimp Mogo and the Loch Ness Monster! What a cracking adventure!" whooped GGH, and he leapt into the air like a footballer when his team scores the winning goal.

Sam stared.

"I'm dreaming," he muttered.

He blinked.

And stared again.

He glanced up to see two very blue eyes looking at him.

He knew those eyes!

And he knew those socks!

There was no mistake, he'd got a clear view when GGH went leaping up.

What should he do?

It felt like his most important decision, ever.

But before he could decide, the door opened and Ms Macaby came in.

Sam sat in a daze while Ms Macaby wittered on.

"I'm sorry I've been so long, Mr Higgins. I do hope they've been taking care of you," she said.

"They've been the greatest, Ms Macaby."

Ms Macaby looked like the cat who'd eaten all the cream. "Yes, they're rather special. I knew that I could count on them."

Ms Macaby smiled her best smile. "I'm a Chimp Mogo fan too, Mr Higgins. My favourite story's the one about the Ghost Invaders. I've always wanted to meet a ghost. I don't suppose I ever shall," she sighed. "But then—" *smile! smile!* "I never thought I'd meet you, either!"

Huh! thought Sam. If only she knew!

"There's a question I'd like to ask," Ms Macaby smiled on. "What does the G. G. stand for? I always thought it was Gloria Georgina." She gave a little laugh. "But of course I was wrong."

"It could be Gloria Georgina for all I know," grinned GGH. "I got the name out of the phone book."

Andy Roberts's hand shot up.

"What's your real name, GGH?"

GGH paused. "There's someone here who can tell you," he said at last. "Tell them, Sam."

Sam saw a blue eye wink at him.

"You're our Mr Brett," he burst out.

As he spoke, off came the beard!

Off came the hat!

"Sam's right," said Mr Brett. "I'm G. G. Higgins."

Chapter 8

"Simmer down! Please! Everyone!"
said Mr Brett.

But there was such excitement at
the discovery of:

> THE TRUE IDENTITY OF
> G. G. HIGGINS

that it was five minutes before the
class was quiet.

"At last!" said Mr Brett. "Well spotted, Sam. You spotted the spotted socks."

"Are those your GGH socks?" asked Jasu.

Mr Brett nodded. "I always wear them when I'm in a GGH mood. I didn't think anyone would notice. But I knew I was rumbled when I saw Sam staring at them."

"I wasn't going to give you away, Mr Brett. I'd decided."

"I knew I could trust you, Sam. But I felt I should own up."

"You should wear that wig and beard all the time," put in Andy Roberts.

"I asked for that, I suppose," said Mr Brett. He looked towards Ms Macaby. "Are you feeling all right?" he asked.

All through the uproar, Ms Macaby had stood in a daze, staring at Mr Brett as if he had three heads. She hadn't said a word. Now at last she found her voice.

"I've heard that writers can do strange things but this is totally beyond me!" she flustered. "Why didn't you tell us before that you were G. G. Higgins? Why be GGH at all?"

"I needed a name to hide behind in case children didn't like what I wrote. I didn't want them going Yawn! Yawn! whenever they saw me. And when the stories took off – well, I was stuck with G. G. Higgins!"

But Ms Macaby was still puzzled about why he'd come as GGH to talk to the class. "You talk to them every day."

"Yes, as Mr Brett. But it was as GGH that I needed their help. I was desperate for another adventure for Chimp Mogo and I hoped if we did lots of Chimp Mogo projects and then I came along as GGH that somewhere, somehow, I might find a new idea."

"And you did!" burst out the class. They were all looking at Sam. He felt himself glowing inside with pride. He hoped his head wasn't swelling too!

"I nearly lost my nerve," grinned Mr Brett. "I nearly *did* go home. Just as well I didn't, eh, Sam?"

Sam took a breath.

Out came the question he was burning to ask:

"Will the Loch Ness Monster really be Chimp Mogo's next adventure?"

Mr Brett nodded. "Surely will," he said, in his G. G. Higgins voice. "You got me out of Big T trouble, Sam. Thanks a million."

Sam stood up.

Hunched his shoulders.

Put his hands in his pockets.

"That's okay, Kiddo."

He sloped off towards the door.

"I'm Mogo, the chimp who does what he does when it has to be done."

He turned and gave a wave. "Right here in the now, I'm off to find the Loch Ness Monster."

When he looked back, the class was following behind. All in their Chimp Mogo masks!

Chapter 9

The following Monday morning:

Yellow socks! thought Sam as Mr Brett walked in.

Was Mr Brett in a good mood?

Was he ever!

"I started a new story last night," he said.

"Has Chimp Mogo found the Loch

Ness Monster already?" asked the class.

Mr Brett shook his head. "Not yet. But he's on the trail. This is a different story."

"I haven't got a title for it yet," Mr Brett went on, "but it's about a boy called Sam. One day he sees that his teacher is wearing orange socks with purple spots..."

"Then what?"

"I'll need some help with what happens next. Any ideas?"

Every hand in the class shot up.

But Sam's hand was up first!

The End